INVISIBLE
BROTHER

CATNIP BOOKS
Published by Catnip Publishing Ltd.
14 Greville Street
London EC1N 8SB

This edition published 2010
1 3 5 7 9 10 8 6 4 2

Text copyright © Pete Johnson, 2010
Illustrations copyright © Mike Gordon, 2010

The moral rights of the author and illustrator have been asserted.

A CIP catalogue record of this book is available from the British Library

ISBN 978-1-846471-01-8

Printed in Poland

Contents

1. A Secret Wish

'Harry,' I said. 'Shut your great, big mouth.'

'You're so rude, Jamie,' he bleated.

'And you're totally annoying. You haven't stopped talking since we left home. Going on and on about all the cups you've won for running.'

'But that's highly interesting.'

'Not when you're telling me for the hundred and fortieth time.' I replied.

And I yawned loudly.

'All right then,' Harry said, 'I'll never say another word to you again.'

'That's the best news I've heard for ages,' I replied.

It was Saturday morning and Harry and I had been sent to the shops to get some extra nosh for the birthday party we were having this afternoon for my best friend Reema. We were on the way home now and Harry had actually stopped talking for a brilliant, fantastic – twenty seconds.

Then he said that he wanted to hold the shopping bag.

'No, I'm holding it,' I said, 'as I'm the eldest.'

'But don't forget, Jamie, that I'm the biggest,' cried Harry, triumphantly.

That was true. Harry was two years younger than me and a whole half a head taller. I can't tell you how much I hated that.

Then Harry went on, 'Actually, I think the person who has won the most cups should carry the bag. So how many have you won?'

I didn't reply. No need. Harry knew the answer. NONE! I'd never won a cup for anything, while his bedroom was

crammed with cups and certificates.

But I had one thing, which Harry didn't.

A magic cape.

I'd just found it one day lying in the branches of a tree. It's dark blue with bright gold around the sides. And at first I just used to pretend I could do magic when I was wearing it. But then I discovered it really can grant wishes. Only you've got to be careful not to make too many wishes at once, otherwise it uses up all the magic for a while.

And here's another very important rule: the cape can only grant wishes when the magic part of it is wet. That's why I always carry a small bottle of water with me. You never know when you might need to make an emergency wish.

Meanwhile, Harry was still jabbering on and on about how he should be allowed to carry the bag as he was bigger than me, and stronger than me and better at every sport than me. On and on he went until I couldn't take anymore.

I decided I was going to make a wish right now – this was definitely an emergency. But I didn't want Harry to spot me doing this.

So I handed the shopping bag to him. 'All right, Harry, you can carry it.'

He looked very surprised and very pleased. 'What . . . well, I'm glad you saw sense. I am, of course, the right person to hold this bag as I'm far stronger than you. In fact, I'm far better at everything than you.'

I watched as Harry pulled open the bag and started peeking inside. 'Oooh, look at all these delicious cakes . . .'

Once Harry got talking about food you couldn't stop him. Maybe that's the reason he's grown so fast – he's always thinking about what he's going to eat next.

He was so busy thinking of all the treats inside the shopping bag that he didn't even notice as I sneaked my magic cape out from my jacket pocket.

It's so silky and soft that it folds up

really small. I also slipped out my small
bottle of water and squirted the Number
Seven, which you'll find inside the collar.
It's funny how this seven always glows
and shines as if it has just been
polished. It is just bursting with magic.

Harry was still busy daydreaming about
food, '. . . jelly frogs, my favourite, I think

I'll eat them first and after that I'll have some chocolate . . .'

Then I put my thumb firmly on the Number Seven and whispered. 'I wish that Harry's voice would change to a very tiny, very squeaky one.'

2. Harry's new voice

Suddenly Harry noticed me putting my cape back in my pocket.

'Did you just make a wish?' he demanded.

'Yes, I did.'

'So what did you wish for?' he asked.

Then he hiccupped, only it came out as a fizzing noise that whizzed up into the air and popped.

'Oh, you'll find out,' I grinned, 'any second now.'

'What do you mean . . .' he began, and then stopped in alarm. His voice had suddenly become similar to that of a little wind-up doll: high-pitched and very hard to hear.

'My voice,' he gasped.

'Sorry, can't hear you,' I said. 'Try and speak up a bit.'

But then out came this tiny, weenie, voice again. 'I can't, because you've put a spell on me, haven't you?'

'That's right – and by the way, I like your new voice so much better than your old one.' I grabbed the shopping bag, 'I think the person with the loudest, deepest voice should carry the bag. And oh, what a surprise – that's me.'

Suddenly Harry rushed forward and tried to grab the cape out of my jacket pocket. But I was too quick for him and darted away.

'I hate you,' he squeaked. His face was all red and he looked really really mad.

'Sorry, can't hear a word you say,' I cried, 'and it's brilliant!'

Harry gave this cry of exasperation, only he sounded like a little bird chirping. Then Mrs Hudson, one of our neighbours, walked past.

'Hello, Jamie,' she cried.

'Hi, Mrs Hudson,' I bellowed back.

'And hello, Harry,' she said.

Harry made this tiny, little noise in reply. She stared at him in some alarm.

'Are you all right, dear?'

'Not really,' he squeaked.

You could tell Mrs Hudson couldn't quite hear him.

'That's a nasty cold you've got,' she said. 'You sound as if you should be at home in bed,' she added, walking hastily away from him.

I smiled. 'Just wait until you go home

and start talking like that. And what
about when you go to school?'

Harry looked at me in alarm. 'You
wouldn't keep the spell on me all
that time.'

'Oh yes I would,' I grinned. But I was
only messing about. I wouldn't really.

Only then Harry burst into tears.

21

'Oh, stop being a cry baby,' I said.

'I hate you,' he squeaked. 'You're the meanest, slimiest, most horrible brother in the whole world.'

I replied. 'Ah, but if you want me to break the spell you've got to say. "Please change me back, *best* brother in the whole world."'

'I'm never saying that,' cried Harry.

'Well, you'll go on being Mr Squeaky Voice then.'

Harry started crying again.

'Don't make such a fuss, you big sissy,' I cried.

I grabbed the cape and said, 'Number Seven, I want you to have my brother talking in his normal, highly annoying voice again.'

Then I waited.

'You'd better be able to change my voice back,' Harry squealed. 'I hope the magic isn't all USED UP.' Suddenly it was as if the volume had been switched right up, and there was Harry shouting away once more.

Only he wasn't the least bit grateful for me changing his voice back. Instead he started punching me.

'What are you doing that for?' I demanded, as I dodged his fists.

'Because you shouldn't play mean tricks like that on me,' he cried.

'Well, you should stop showing off all the time,' I said.

'You're only jealous,' he cried. 'And I don't want to talk to you any more.'

Then he stood at the top of this very long, very hilly lane, with his arms folded. 'I'm not going home with you.'

'So what are you going to do instead?' I asked.

'Don't know. I might just stand here for a few hours,' he said.

'That sounds so boring.'

'Don't care. I just want to get away from you,' he cried. 'So, goodbye.'

'Mum will go mad if we're not back soon,' I said.

'Don't care,' shouted Harry again.

And then this van rumbled past us. It stopped a couple of doors down the lane. We watched a delivery man leap out and rush up the drive. He was carrying a massive parcel.

'I wonder what's in there?' I said.

Harry forgot about our argument for a moment and said, 'I bet it's something really exciting, like a . . .' And then he let out a shriek of horror.

'Look, Look!

Then I saw it too.

The delivery man couldn't have put the brakes on properly because the van was now moving all by itself down the hill. That was bad enough, but at the end of the slope there was a little boy playing in the road.

'Get out of the way,' yelled Harry.

'Yeah, move now,' I shouted.

But the boy didn't even look up.

'He can't hear us,' said Harry, 'and he could get . . . squashed.'

'So we've got to do something,' I cried, 'and fast!'

3. The Runaway Van

Suddenly Harry leapt forward and snatched the cape out of my pocket.

'Hey,' I began.

But Harry was already crying, 'Number Seven, make me the fastest runner in the whole world.' Then he flung the cape at me and charged off down the road.

For the first few metres he ran quickly –

Harry is a fast runner anyway and has even won cups for it, you know. (Yawn, yawn.)

But suddenly the magic started working – and Harry raced off so fast it was like watching a speeded up film. His feet really didn't seem to touch the ground.

Two boys rushed up and stood watching

Harry, open-mouthed.

'Is he an awesome runner or what?' said the first one.

'Do you know him?' the other boy turned and asked me.

'A bit,' I admitted. 'He's my brother.' And I couldn't help a note of pride slipping into my voice.

I started running down the road as well. So did the two boys, but we were nowhere near as fast as Harry, of course.

Then the boys and I gave a loud cheer. Harry had reached the van. But he still had to stop it, as the van went on hurtling nearer and nearer to the little boy.

Was Harry going to be in time?

Harry quickly wrenched open the driver's door and jumped inside. His head just reached above the steering wheel of the van. And, of course, he'd never actually driven a car in his life before. But he knew how the brakes worked all right. He slammed them on so fiercely they gave a loud groan.

The van rocked to a halt right in front of the little boy.

The boy looked up for the first time and saw how close the van was to him.

But he didn't seem scared or anything.

Instead, he clapped his hands as if he'd just watched an amazing trick – and laughed.

A woman came rushing up, obviously his mother.

'Oh Robin, there you are. I've been looking for you everywhere.' Then she saw Harry clamber out of the driver's seat of the lorry. 'What are you . . . ?' she began.

All at once she noticed how very close the van was to Robin. Her face turned the palest you've ever seen.

'What's happened?' she gasped.

Harry started explaining. Then the two boys and me rushed over and joined in too. I thought Robin's mother was going to faint with shock. Instead she swayed forward and picked up her son.

'You naughty boy,' she said to him. 'I can't believe you just wandered off whilst I was talking on the phone. I couldn't see you anywhere! If this boy hadn't raced to your rescue . . .' she shuddered. 'You must be a very fast runner,' she said to Harry.

'Oh, I am,' agreed Harry.

'The fastest we've ever seen,' agreed the two boys.

Of course, Harry was lapping up all this attention.

Then the driver of the van came puffing towards us. 'I couldn't believe my eyes when I saw my van had gone,' he spluttered, his face swimming in sweat. 'The brake must have slipped –

yes, that's what happened. Well, you did very well, son. Thank you very much.'

Harry's smile got even broader.

But then Robin's mother shrieked at the driver. 'You're totally irresponsible!'

'What about you?' shouted the van driver. 'Fancy letting this little lad go walking off on his own?'

'I did nothing of the sort . . .' began the woman.

'Look,' I interrupted, 'the main thing is, that, er . . . Robin is all right.'

'And all because I saved him,' added Harry, not very modestly. Still this calmed everyone down.

Robin's mother invited us round for a meal and said to Harry, 'I can never thank you enough.'

And the driver of the van shook Harry by the hand four times. He finally drove off with two loud blasts of his horn, while the two boys clambered round Harry.

'You're a real hero,' said one. He was called Fraser and was older than me. He was also gigantic, nearly as tall as my dad. I'd seen him around and always found him and all his mates a bit scary.

The other boy was called Russ. He was tall and very skinny with ginger hair. They'd never bothered even saying 'Hello' to Harry and me before.

They were soon ignoring me again, but they were chatting away to Harry all right. Then they started whispering. They obviously didn't want me to hear.

Well, I didn't care. I turned away from them. I had no interest in their stupid conversation anyhow.

Finally Mum rang on my mobile, wanting to know where we were. I called over to Harry and the boys. 'Mum says we've got to come home this very second.'

Harry sped over to me in the blink of an eye, beaming away. 'It's great being a hero,' he announced.

'You shouldn't have used my cape

without asking first,' I said, putting it in my jacket pocket again.

'I was in a rush, though,' said Harry. 'And as I'm already a very fast runner, I thought the magic wouldn't have to work so hard. Also,' he grinned cheekily, 'you wouldn't have been able to see above the steering wheel, would you? You're so much smaller than me.'

I managed to ignore this and said, 'Well anyway, you saved Robin all right, with the massive help of my cape.'

'So do I get a reward now?' asked Harry.

'From who?' I demanded.

'From you. Let me borrow your cape for the rest of the day.'

'No way!'

'Oh, go on, don't be tight. I deserve a reward.'

I stared at him. 'Well, there's no way I'll let you have my cape for a whole day. But you can have one wish now.'

'Only one?' said Harry indignantly.

'Yeah, that's it. Take it or leave it.'

'I'll take it,' said Harry.

I pulled the cape out of my pocket and squirted some fresh water on Number Seven.

'Right, you can wish,' I said. Harry put his hand on Number Seven. But I still kept hold of the cape too. I wouldn't put it past Harry to run off with it.

Harry closed his eyes and said. 'Number Seven, please give me a bar of chocolate which never ends, so that as soon as you've eaten one bar, another one appears immediately.'

'But Number Seven,' I added. 'Please make this spell last for just today.'

Harry glared at me. 'Why did you say that?'

'Because you'll only make yourself sick if you eat a million bars of chocolate every day.'

'I wouldn't eat a million bars of chocolate a day,' said Harry. 'Three quarters of a million, maybe, but no more.'

The next moment a large bar of chocolate came whooshing out of the air, landing by Harry's feet. 'Cheers Number Seven,' said Harry.

Then he picked it up and took a massive bite.

'Mmm,' he said appreciatively. 'This is delicious.'

He offered the bar to me. And he was right. The chocolate was the best I'd ever tasted. It just melted in your mouth. Not that I was surprised. You only ever get the best from my magic cape.

As soon as we'd finished that bar another immediately took its place, the fattest bar of chocolate you'd ever seen – like a chocolate balloon – and that was equally tasty.

Harry sighed happily. 'This has been the best Saturday of my life. I mean, it's not even eleven o'clock yet and already I've saved a boy from a runaway van, got my own magic bar of chocolate and been asked to join a secret gang.'

I gaped at him. 'You mean those two boys who were here?'

'That's right, Fraser and Russ, my two new mates.'

'But they're years older than you – they're even older than me.'

'I know,' said Harry, 'and I did especially

ask them if they wanted you to join too. But they said no, only me. Sorry.'

'I don't care,' I replied. 'I never wanted to be in their gang anyway.'

'I can't tell you where their den is,' went on Harry. 'Well, all I can say is, it's in an old deserted hut somewhere, but I can't even tell you one more thing about it. Sorry.'

Then he added excitedly. 'I'm going to my first meeting this afternoon. Try and not be too jealous, won't you?'

'Me, jealous of you?' I said, through gritted teeth, 'I've got a magic cape – and you haven't. Never forget that.'

4. My Cape Vanishes

Mum was cross when we arrived back so late with the shopping. 'Wherever have you been?' she asked.

'You won't believe what happened,' cried Harry. 'I'm a hero now as I . . .'

'I haven't got time for one of your stories, Harry,' said Mum briskly. 'Aunt Nora will be here any minute, and I've got to leave everything ready for her.'

Mum and Dad were going off to visit some old friends. Aunt Nora, who was really my mum's aunt, so very old indeed, would be looking after us, as well as Reema when she came round for her birthday party later that afternoon.

I went off to call for Reema. To my surprise Harry said he wanted to come too.

'Why?' I asked.

'Because I want to wish Reema a very happy birthday,' said Harry.

'Well you can't,' I said.

'Oh, let him go with you,' said Mum. 'It's nice he wants to see your friend.'

'No, it isn't,' I said.

I decided Harry just wanted to show off about him being a hero.

I knocked on Reema's door. She

answered and looked very pleased to see me. Some people are surprised that my best friend is a girl. But you couldn't find a better one. You can tell her anything. And she's the only person, apart from Harry and me, who knows about the magic cape.

'Happy birthday and all that rhubarb,' I said. 'This is for you, by the way.' And I flung my present at her.

'You shouldn't have,' she said. 'But I'm very glad you did.'

'Open it then,' said Harry, dancing

about excitedly. He was standing very close to me, but I was too busy watching to see if Reema liked her present to worry about him.

She gave a laugh of delight when she saw what it was – a computer game. 'Oh, this is exactly what I wanted,' she said. 'You are clever.'

'I know,' I murmured. She'd been talking about that game for ages.

'It's just a perfect present, isn't it, Harry?' She looked up, and I turned round. We both noticed at the same moment – Harry had gone.

'Why did he just run off like that?' I asked.

'I don't know,' cried Reema.

I reached into my pocket and let out a

cry of horror. 'My magic cape,' I gasped. 'It's gone.'

5. The Spooky Cough

I was so angry with Harry I thought my head would explode.

While I paced around Reema's garden I quickly explained what had happened that morning. 'He's stolen my cape! And you know why?' Before she could answer I went on. 'So he can show off to those boys who want him to join their gang. At this minute he's probably telling them all about my magic cape.

I'll never, ever see it again.'

'Of course you will,' said Reema as she paced with me.

'And I don't have a clue where the gang's den is. So I'll never find it.' My lip started to tremble. 'That cape is the only special thing about me.'

'That's not true at all,' said Reema, patting me on the shoulder. 'You're my best friend for a start. So that makes you incredibly special.'

I stopped walking and gave her a smile so my trembly lip had something else to do.

Then Reema's mum came out.

'Isn't Aunt Nora expecting you for one o'clock?' she said, looking at her watch. 'It's ten past already, off you go!'

As we set off for my house Reema said brightly, 'We don't know for certain Harry is with that gang. He might have just taken your cape for a joke. And he could be back home again now. You know how Harry loves his food.'

'Yeah but he loves annoying me even more,' I muttered. 'He won't be at home.'

I was right.

When we arrived home Aunt Nora's first question was. 'Where's Harry? I thought he was with you.'

'He was,' I said angrily, 'but then he just ran off.'

Aunt Nora tutted. 'Well, we shan't wait for him . . . and there'll be more food for you two, won't there?' Then she added, 'Harry can be so naughty, can't he?'

'Naughty,' I muttered. 'And annoying and sneaky and . . .'

Reema smiled across at me. 'He'll be back soon, you'll see.'

The food did cheer me up a little. It was an amazing selection of cakes, crisps, jellies and sandwiches. Reema and I ate and ate.

'You just wait until you see what we've got for your actual birthday party later,' I said. But all the time I was listening out for Harry to come home.

'Well, you haven't left much food for Harry, have you?' said Aunt Nora, bustling in.

We'd left Harry just one pot of jelly, one sandwich and one crisp, but no cake. People who steal magic capes don't deserve cake.

'I wonder where he is. I shall have something to say to him when he does turn up,' Aunt Nora carried on. Then she suddenly smiled. 'But it's lovely to see you all again.'

Aunt Nora was rather absent minded but I was very pleased to see her too.

Suddenly we heard this very loud cough outside the front door. It made us all jump. Then there came a second, even louder cough.

'Whoever is doing that?' cried Aunt Nora. She rushed to the front door with me and Reema following her.

We were right by the door when whoever it was coughed again. We all looked at each other. Why hadn't they rung the bell?

Aunt Nora shrugged and opened the door. 'Hello, can I – oh.'

No one was there.

She looked around for a bit then shut the door.

'Someone playing a silly joke,' said Aunt Nora. 'Well, I'll be in the garden for a few minutes if anyone needs me.'

Aunt Nora loves our garden. Although she says we should get a garden gnome. I could never look a garden gnome in the face again.*

Reema and I went inside and sat down again. 'That cough was so spooky,' she said.

I agreed.

And then we heard that cough again. Only this time it was in the room with us – right next to Reema!

Reema clutched my arm.

'Who's there?' we cried together.

'Don't be alarmed, it's only me,' hissed a voice I recognised instantly.

* See Bug Brother for the full story.

'Harry,' I cried. 'Where are you hiding?'

I leapt up and opened the nearest cupboard, then peeked under the table, ready to drag Harry out of his stupid hiding place.

'I'm not hiding anywhere,' he said. 'I'm standing right beside you.' Then he added, 'But I'm afraid there's been a little accident.'

6. My Invisible Brother

'You mean you're invisible,' said Reema.

'Yes,' he whispered.

'But how – and where's my cape?' I cried.

Harry gave a little sob. 'Oh, you won't believe what's happened.'

'Just tell us,' said Reema.

'And you'd better know where my cape is,' I added. 'You did steal it, didn't you?'

'No, I only borrowed it to have with me when I went off to meet the gang in their secret den.' said Harry. 'And I showed them my bar of chocolate, which never runs out.'

'You total idiot,' I cried. If I could have seen where he was standing, then I'd have thumped him.

Harry gulped. 'But they were so fascinated by it. They said it was the coolest thing they've ever seen. They took it off me and wouldn't give it back. They said I had to tell them how it worked if I wanted to be in ther gang.'

'Oh no,' I groaned and sat back down in my chair with a thud. Reema gave me a comforting pat on the back.

'Go on, Harry,' she said.

'But I *didn't*! I thought they might take the cape off me too. That's when they stopped being friendly and started shouting at me. And then . . .' he let out another sob, 'they said if I didn't tell them how I'd got the magic chocolate bar I'd get mashed.'

'Poor you,' gasped Reema and reached

out to give him a comforting pat too. Only she missed.

'What!' I shouted. ' "Poor Harry", you've got to be joking.' Reema gave me a look and I tried to calm down a little. 'So tell us what you did next.'

'Well,' said Harry, 'I saw my chance and I ran away. I can still run magically fast, but I couldn't remember where to go and I could hear them charging after me and I slipped, didn't I? Luckily the grass was still a bit wet after the rain, so I rubbed the cape over it, and then wished to be invisible. It was the first thing I could think of. I wasn't sure if the cape was wet enough for the magic to work at first. So I started running once more. Only I slipped.' He paused.

'And?' I said, feeling worried.

Harry's voice was really quiet when he replied, 'And I dropped your cape, Jamie.'

I let out a huge groan.

'And,' concluded Harry, 'that was when I realised I was invisible. It was quite funny, seeing them searching everywhere for me and not able to work out how I'd vanished.' He gave a nervous little laugh. 'But I'm afraid they've got the chocolate bar *and* the magic cape.'

I glared into the air. 'You're such a big show off,' I shouted.

'I know,' whispered Harry. 'It's just I was so pleased they wanted to be friends with me after they saw me save that boy, and I thought how can I make them like me even more . . . that's why I told them about the chocolate and then . . .'

'Showed them the cape you stole from your brother . . .' I interrupted.

'No, I told you I only borrowed it,' said Harry. 'And I didn't show them it. I would have brought it back, only now . . .'

'My cape's with that gang. And if I can't get it back you'll stay my invisible brother forever.'

Harry started to cry very loudly.

'Sssh,' I said. 'You'll only bring Aunt Nora back.'

'I don't care,' said Harry.

'Oh don't be too hard on him,' said

Reema. 'He's had a horrible time.' She walked over to where all the noise was coming from and tried to give Harry an encouraging squeeze.

'What!' I spluttered. 'Well, that's typical, isn't it? Harry never gets blamed for anything.'

'It's not that,' said Reema. 'It's just Harry is so unhappy. Look.'

I could see where his tears had made

damp patches on her shoulder.

'I really am,' Harry agreed.

'And he's obviously sorry, too.' Reema added.

'I really, really am.' I couldn't see if he was nodding as well.

'Good,' I said. 'If you're that sorry, then you won't mind me having your iPod. As you're invisible you won't be able to see where your ears are to put the earphones in anyway. And I might take your favourite cap. Well, you won't need it any more, if you put it on, it would only turn invisible like the rest of you.'

'Oh, stop teasing him,' said Reema. 'I've just had one of my dead-crazy, dead-brilliant ideas!'

7. Reema's Plan

Well, come on then,' I said to Reema. 'Tell us this dead-crazy, dead-brilliant idea.'

Reema leant forward. 'Harry shows us where the gang's secret den is. Then I knock on the door and ask the gang something. While I'm talking to them Harry slips inside. Then he starts moving stuff about, so the gang think their den is haunted. They run out screaming with fear. Harry grabs the cape, wets it and he is the invisible boy no longer.' Reema grinned triumphantly. 'Isn't that the best plan you've ever heard?'

'It really is,' said Harry. 'And I'm *so* sick of being invisible.'

'I don't know,' I said. 'I think it's great not having to see your ugly face all the time.'

'I'm not ugly,' cried Harry indignantly.

'Don't start arguing,' said Reema, 'Let's go.'

'Could you just get me some food first? I'm absolutely starving,' said Harry.

'You can't be,' I said. 'Not after all the bars of chocolate you've scoffed.'

'I tell you, being invisible really gives you an appetite,' cried Harry.

I went into the kitchen and found two left-over sandwiches and brought them in to Harry.

I felt a soft breeze as Harry snatched them from me. For a second the sandwiches just hung in the air. Then Harry must have taken a massive bite, as half of one of the sandwiches just vanished. And then the other half disappeared.

Only one little piece of sandwich remained hovering in the air when Aunt Nora rushed in.

'I'm getting worried about Harry . . .' she began.

Then she stopped and gaped at the

piece of sandwich floating about all by itself.

'Eat it,' I muttered to Harry.

But instead he had to be silly, didn't he? And Harry made the sandwich roll round and round with his invisible hand.

Aunt Nora's eyes widened. 'Look at that,' she gasped.

But at last the sandwich disappeared, wolfed down by Harry.

'Look at what, Aunt Nora?' I asked.

'I thought . . .' her eyes started to blink furiously. 'I thought – oh, never mind, my eyes must be playing tricks on me again. Now, what was I going to say to you? Oh yes, I'm worried about Harry.'

'We think we know where he is,' I said. 'And we're off to get him right now.'

Reema added, 'He'll be back before you know it.'

'So see you soon, Aunt Nora,' cried Harry.

Aunt Nora actually jumped into the air with shock. 'Did you hear that?'

Reema and I smiled ever so innocently at her. 'Hear what Aunt Nora?' I said.

'I thought I heard Harry.' Aunt Nora frowned and looked about. 'But how could I have? A good rest, that's what I need. I've been doing too much.'

She sped off while Reema said to Harry, 'You are so naughty, Harry! Your poor Aunt.'

'I know but I just couldn't resist it,' said Harry. 'Did you see her face when I suddenly spoke? That really cheered me up.'

We set off in quite good spirits with Harry whispering directions to us, since we couldn't see to follow him. He led us through the wood. It was a bright, October day. We sloshed through the leaves which had fallen everywhere. But otherwise everything seemed very quiet and still.

Hidden away in the middle of the woods was an old hut, rotting away.

'Sssh,' whispered Harry. 'They're in there.' All the windows had boards over them. But one of them had a tiny crack. I peeked inside.

There were a group of boys – the two we'd seen this morning and two others – all clustered round my cape.

My cape!

They were chanting words over it too, trying to cast spells.

'They know it's magic. Look at them,' I cried. Reema and Harry crammed around to peer inside as well.

'But they don't know the cape only works when it's wet,' said Harry.

'Not yet, they don't,' I said. 'But they

could accidentally find out. Oh, if I could see you right now I'd punch you so hard.'

'I told you I'm sorry,' he cried.

'Keep your voices down,' said Reema with a gulp. 'Look, we're going to put my brilliant plan into action and then we'll have the cape back. So here goes,' she added.

I think she was trying to sound more confident than she felt. 'Harry, get ready to rush in . . .'

'I'm right beside you,' he said. 'And as soon as that door opens I'll whizz inside and cause total chaos.'

'And Jamie, go and hide!' said Reema. I did as I was told and went round the corner of the hut.

Reema knocked sharply on the door.

After a few seconds it opened, but only a tiny bit. 'Can you help me please,' cried Reema. 'I'm lost.'

The boy opened it a little more. Two more boys joined him, staring out very suspiciously. They were the ones we'd seen earlier when Harry saved the little boy from the runaway lorry. And one of them, Fraser, had my cape in his hand.

I was so angry about this I nearly sprang forward. I wondered if I could snatch the cape away from him. I'd have to move with lightning speed but I bet I could do it. I edged even closer.

Meanwhile, Reema was saying. 'I just don't know how to get home. I'm totally lost.'

I think the boys were starting to believe
her story when, very unfortunately, one of
them spotted me.

'It's him, Harry's brother,' Fraser called. 'Get him.'

And before I knew what was happening I was surrounded by all four boys in the gang. They were all much bigger than me.

'What are you doing here?' demanded Russ, who seemed to be the leader.

'Nothing much, I was just having a look round. Sorry to disturb you.'

'Did Harry send you here?' asked one of the boys suddenly. 'To try and get the magic cape back?'

'Magic cape, what are you talking about?' I tried to laugh, but my throat was dry.

'I think,' said Russ, 'that cape can grant wishes. I just need to know how it works.

Maybe you can tell me.'

'Not me,' I said.

Russ frowned. 'Let's take him into the hut as our hostage – her too,' he added, as Reema was watching all this in horror.

As we were pushed inside the shed she whispered to me, 'Why didn't you stay hidden?'

'Sorry,' I croaked back, 'but I had a plan of my own.'

'Not a very good one.' Reema was smiling, but I could tell she was worried.

Their den was dark and cold and smelt of dust and stale air. The four boys stood round Reema and me. 'Now start talking,' said Fraser. 'What are you doing here?'

'I told you . . .' I began.

'No,' snapped Fraser. 'None of that you were going for a nature ramble rubbish. Tell us the real reason you –' Suddenly he stopped talking.

For a couple of seconds he probably even stopped breathing.

He stood watching, open-mouthed as the magic bar of chocolate floated into the air, gave a little wiggle and then started dive-bombing the gang.

They ducked in horror as this demented chocolate bar came charging towards them. Harry was certainly doing some good work here.

The boys were so shocked they'd even dropped my magic cape. There it lay, agonisingly close to me. I could almost reach out and touch it.

'I'm getting out of here,' said one boy.

There was a mass scramble to the door as the chocolate bar continued circling round the room, like a demented wasp.

Suddenly Russ called out, 'Stop!' And then he looked right at me. 'You're making the chocolate bar do this, aren't you?'

I was about to deny it when I suddenly had an idea. 'Yes, it is me. I can do magic all by myself.'

The boys stared at me – half-impressed, half-disbelieving.

'Chocolate bar, sit down now,' I said. Immediately Harry stopped running about and the chocolate bar fell to the ground.

'Now, if you open the door,' I said,

'I will show you a truly incredible piece of magic.'

'It's a trick,' called out someone.

But I could see they were also very keen to see what I was going to do.

'Don't let them run away,' said Russ. And two of the boys surrounded Reema and me. 'But open the door – let's see what he can do.'

They slowly opened the door and I cried out. 'Get ready to see the most amazing magic trick of your whole life.'

8. I Become a Magician

Everyone was watching me really carefully now. I gave a nervous cough and then cried. 'Cape, rise up into the air.'

Right away the cape started to soar off the ground. Of course, it was really just Harry lifting it up. But it did look as if I'd brought the cape to life. Harry wiggled it slightly and all of them – even Russ – watched open-mouthed.

'Now cape,' I said, 'I want you to fly away as fast as you can.'

The cape didn't need telling twice. It sped out of that den. But all the boys were still gawping at me.

'What are you?' asked Russ.

'Me?' I replied. 'I'm a magician. And if you annoy me any more I will put a spell on you.'

'He will too,' said Reema. 'Once he turned his aunt into a garden gnome. I have never forgotten that.'

'But why did you do that?' asked Fraser.

'Just felt like it,' I said. Enjoying myself now I went on, 'How would you like to be a garden gnome?'

'I really wouldn't,' said Fraser hastily.

'Well, just watch out and don't get him mad,' said Reema. 'When he gets angry . . . you don't know what he'll do.'

She and I started walking towards the door. I whirled round. 'Anyone want to stop us leaving?' I asked.

No one spoke at first.

Then Russ said in this odd, husky voice. 'No, you can go.'

What a great moment that was. A whole gang of boys – years older and all scared of ME!

I just floated towards the open doorway, Reema beside me. And that's when something totally unexpected happened, which ruined everything.

For I felt something rush past me and back inside the shed.

It was the cape.

9. Follow That Cape!

Reema and I whirled round in total horror.

What was Harry playing at? Why had he come back?

I was so shocked I blurted out. 'What are you doing here?'

'Forgot my special chocolate bar. And I can't go home without that,' replied Harry.

And even though no one could see

Harry, everyone was able to hear him all right.

'What's going on?' asked Russ.

'Do not dare to question me,' I said, 'Or I will turn you into something deeply horrible.'

'He really will,' added Reema.

But the spell had been broken. 'What's going on here?' asked Russ again.

'This is some kind of stupid trick,' said Fraser. He made as if to grab the cape.

'Do not dare touch that cape,' I cried in my deepest, strongest voice.

Fraser jumped back as if he'd just been bitten. And the cape, with the chocolate bar now flying right beside it, dived out of the hut.

But they weren't going to give up that easily. Suddenly Russ cried, 'Follow that cape.'

And all four of the boys charged outside.

I turned to Reema. 'Oh why did Harry have to come back?'

'And why did you have to talk to him?' she added.

'Well, he caught me by surprise, didn't he?' I said. 'Anyway, what are we going to do now?'

'Follow that cape,' said Reema.

So we joined the boys thundering after it through the woods. Not one of them had caught up with the cape yet – Harry still had magically fast feet. But he'd already done a lot of running around and he must have been tired

because the taller, stronger boys were
gaining on him fast.

Then Russ dived forward and grabbed
the chocolate bar. The cape faltered for a
moment.

'No, forget about the chocolate. Keep going,' I yelled.

I thought if Harry could get home ahead of the gang, then he could hurl some water on the cape and make another wish. Maybe he could turn into a GIANT brother and scare off Fraser and Russ and their horrible friends.

As we reached my road Harry put on an extra spurt and raced down the road.

Two women stood watching the cape.

'That's amazing,' said one.

'No, I can see the string,' said the other.

The cape sped into our front garden. But the gang weren't far behind. The cape fluttered around the house, trying to find an open window, which it could squeeze into.

But every window was tightly shut.

So then it flew over the back gate. I heaved a sigh of relief until I realised the gate wasn't locked, and watched all the boys charge through it too.

'Now what's going to happen?' gasped Reema.

10. Extra Guests

Puffing and panting, Reema and I followed everyone else into the back garden.

I heard Aunt Nora cry. 'Oh, have you boys all come for Reema's birthday?'

She can't have seen the magical flying cape.

'Yeah, that's right,' said Russ, waving the chocolate bar in the air. 'We wouldn't want to miss that!'

The boys all started laughing, but Aunt Nora just said, 'How nice. Well, do go in . . . oh, you already have,' she added, as the boys piled past her into the house.

Then Aunt Nora spotted Reema and me.

'Hello, Reema dear, your friends are very early and very enthusiastic too. But not to worry, I'll go and get some orange squash for them.'

Aunt Nora darted into the house and we followed, just in time to hear one of the boys say. 'I bet that cape's upstairs in his bedroom.' They all charged upstairs while I wondered where Harry had really got to.

Then I heard a sharp cry from the kitchen. It sounded like Aunt Nora.

It was.

She stood pointing, with a shaking hand at the sink. 'That tap just switched on all by itself and then your cape flew over, Jamie – and, well, look at it.'

The cape appeared to be having a little shower as it swung about energetically under the tap.

'What is going on?' squealed Aunt Nora, 'Am I going mad?'

'Oh no,' I began, hoping Harry wouldn't turn into a giant after all, that would be too much for poor old Aunt Nora to handle. And then Aunt Nora gave a strange, spluttering noise as a normal-sized Harry just seemed to blast down out of nowhere.

He gave her a friendly wave. 'Hi Aunt Nora, how's tricks?' Poor Aunt Nora gave another scream, and then stuttered. 'But, but, but, where have you come from?'

'Shall we go next door for a minute?' said Reema, putting an arm around Aunt Nora.

'One second Harry's not there, the next he is,' cried Aunt Nora.

'Let's talk about it next door,' said Reema, and then she guided Aunt Nora away, while the boys came thumping down the stairs again.

I seized hold of the wet cape and placed my thumb firmly on the number seven.

'Number Seven, I'd really like it if you made these boys forget everything that's happened over these past six hours, and especially everything about the magic cape.'

As I finished speaking the boys surged in.

Russ glanced at Harry and then said. 'So you're back. Well look, all we want is that magic cape. And I know it's magic, so hand it over, you two.'

Harry and I looked at each other and then stood very close together. 'You'll never get your hands on that cape,' said Harry, 'will they, Jamie?'

'No they won't.'

Fraser loomed menacingly in front of me. 'Oh yes we will.' Then he added, 'It's quite wet.'

'Perhaps it only works when it's wet,' said Russ.

I let out a cry of horror and Russ cried, 'That's it . . . I've discovered the cape's secret, haven't I?'

11. Reema's Party

And so he had.

It was just lucky that the next moment the magic finally started to work. All the boys' eyes blinked furiously as if they were just awakening from a trance.

'What on earth are we doing here?' demanded Russ.

The other boys shrugged.

I slammed my hand against my head. What were we going to tell them?

We'd run out of wishes. My cape could only grant seven wishes at a time and we'd used them all up. Magic couldn't help us this time.

Suddenly, Reema burst through the door and said. 'You've come to my party, haven't you?'

A look of total shock crossed their faces. 'We've come to a girl's party?' cried Russ.

'Yes, isn't it wonderful? We're going to have great fun. Later we might even play a skipping game.'

'What!' yelped Fraser.

'And then we're going to pretend to be princesses. That'll be lovely, won't it?'

'Princesses!' shrieked Russ.

'And then I'm going to tell you my story about a fairy – you do believe in fairies don't you?'

The boys just gaped at her.

Harry and I looked at each other in relief. Trust Reema to think of something brilliant. Then Aunt Nora wandered in.

'Now come on, Reema, don't leave your guests in the kitchen. Take them inside, I'm feeling much better now so I think it's time we got on with your party.'

Four stunned-looking boys tottered into the sitting room, which Aunt Nora had decorated in honour of Reema's birthday.

They sat down very reluctantly. 'Whose idea was it to come here?' asked Russ.

'It must have been yours,' said Fraser. 'You are the leader . . . though you might not be for much longer, bringing us to a soppy girl's ickle, wickle birthday party.'

'I don't get it . . .' began Russ.

Then Reema pranced in again. 'Oh, it's so lovely to see you all here at my party.' She clapped her hands, 'I've got such a wonderful surprise for you all too. After tea I'm going to give each of you a nice big, squelchy, gooey KISS. So who'd like to have a kiss first?'

The boys were so horror-struck, they couldn't speak.

Suddenly Fraser leapt up. 'I'm getting out of here,' he cried. Then all four of them tore out of our house and pelted down the road. While Reema, Harry and myself laughed and laughed.

We laughed about it until Reema had to go home.

Harry and I were still laughing about it at Harry's bedtime.

'I don't know what's got into you all today,' said Mum, who was back in charge now. 'Reema's party must have been great fun. I've never seen Reema so giggly and as for you two, you have just sat chuckling all evening. Well, it's bedtime for you now, Harry.'

'Oh can't I stay up just five more minutes?' said Harry, wiping the tears from his eyes.

'No,' said Mum. 'Off to bed now.'

Harry got up very slowly, very reluctantly. 'What a day!' he cried. I could still hear him laughing as he walked upstairs.

A moment later, Mum came in again. 'Jamie, I found this under one of the chairs. Whose is it?'

It was Harry's magic chocolate bar. It must have fallen out of Russ's pocket when he left. And we'd forgotten all about it.

Suddenly Harry was downstairs again. When food is mentioned, Harry has supersonic hearing.

'Oh, it's mine,' said Harry. 'Can I eat it upstairs?'

Mum looked confused at his sudden arrival, but said, 'You can't still be hungry?'

'Yes I am,' said Harry. 'Please, Mum.'

Mum softened. 'Oh, all right then, but this is the last bar of chocolate you eat tonight, all right?'

'Don't worry Mum,' said Harry, 'I promise this is the last bar of chocolate

I'll eat tonight.' Then he grinned and winked at me.

And I grinned and winked back.

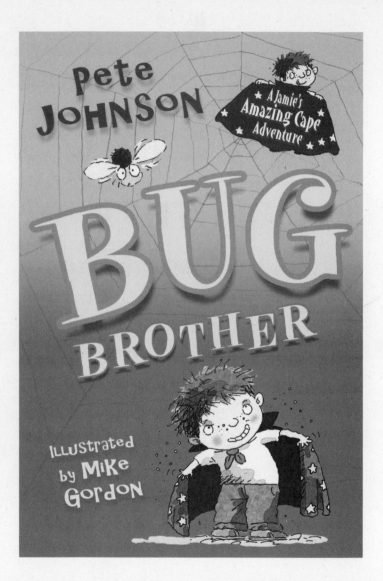

Pete
JOHNSON

A Jamie's
Amazing Cape
Adventure

BUG
BROTHER

ILLUSTRATED
by MiKE
GORDON

FIRST IN THE SERIES

BUG
BROTHER

Jamie is sick of his little brother Harry buzzing around all the time. Harry is like one of those really noisy, annoying bluebottles.

So Jamie makes a wish on his amazing cape and hey presto! Harry's a bluebottle! But how will Jamie turn him back?

ROODICA THE RUDE

by MARGARET RYAN

illustrated by SARAH HORNE

Long ago, when wolves and bears roamed the land,
and before underpants had been invented,
the Romans conquered Britain.

(Romans 1 - Celts 0)

The Romans built fine houses and straight roads,
they encourage the Celts to take baths.

But not everyone liked the Romans. Lots of people
fought back. No one more stubbornly than Queen
Goodica's youngest daughter Roodica the Rude!

SIR QUINTON QUEST

By Kaye Umansky, author of the best selling
Pongwiffy books, illustrated by Judy Brown.

Sir Quinton Quest: world famous explorer, lifelong
member of the Explorers Club, and many-time winner
of the Explorer of the Year Challenge Cup.

Findley Ffoothold: fiendishly good-looking explorer,
successful author and Sir Quinton's arch enemy.
Sir Quinton will do whatever it takes to expose
Ffoothold for the imposter he is – but sometimes his
determination can get in the way of making
the discovery of a lifetime...

You can find out more about other
exciting Catnip books by visiting:
www.catnippublishing.co.uk